SEIYEFA
THE CASSAVA BOY

i

Published in Nigeria in 2020 by Siloko
Oyintari Ben.
Copy right© Siloko Oyintari Ben 2020
.
ISBN- 9781370386505

For more information, contact the author on:

Mobile – 08036029195, 08026007839.
Facebook – @SOB BOOKS
Twitter - @silokooyintariben
Instagram - @sob_books
b l o g   –
www.silokooyintari.blogspot.com

ACKNOWLEDGMENT

To the memory of my father R.B
Siloko (RAMSILO).
Dad, I will remember you always.

To my mother Elizabeth Siloko.
Thanks for all the sacrifices
you have done for me.

SEIYEFA
THE CASSAVA
BOY

By Siloko Oyintari Ben

viii

SEIYEFA
THE CASSAVA
BOY

BY SILOKO OYINTARI BEN

x

I t was a cold November afternoon in 1994 under the mango tree by the waterside. I heard the voice clearly from afar, Seiyefa!!! Seiyefa!!! I didn't bother to answer because my parents told me a very scary tale about spirits calling people sometimes, and if one mistakenly answers in error and doesn't see anyone, they must quickly say *Ine Teme Waibo* [My spirit come back].

Pheeewww! Pheeeeeewww!! Came the sound as my slippers hit a ripe opioro mango which came falling down. This opioro go sweet o, I said. As I was about to pick the mango from the ground so I could taste it and clear my doubt; just then I heard sounds as I looked up and discovered the weather was changing.

The voice kept calling Seiyefa!!! Seiyefa!!! I could hear the thunderstorm loudly each time my name echoed, which made it more frightening.

The bravery in me ignited, being among the best wrestlers in my community. I moved towards the direction of the voice with courage. Just then, my eyes peeped in on Kurotimi, the greatest wrestler in my community – famous with the name, 'the Power house.' I hailed him – Power! But the look on Kurotimi's eyes wasn't pleasant. Immediately, I yelled at him asking *Tei*

Ke Pama? [what happened?]; he was silent, I asked yelling at the top of my voice, Power!!! ***Tei ke pama***? [Power what happened?]

Kurotimi looked into my eyes, hugged me tightly and whispered into my ears, ***General don go battle field and him no dey come back.*** It was as if a different spirit entered me, I held Kurotimi back, as if I was about to shake myself off his grip, I shouted louder at him this time, Power, **ye gba ni dia eh. Gba! Gba!! Gba!!! Gba!!!!** [Power, tell me something, say it, say it, say it] I can see tears rolling down the cheeks of Kurotimi, then I was convinced something was wrong.

Ine dau fi-dou [your father is dead], it was as if the rains were waiting for the news to break. It poured down heavily on us. I tried to run into the river in a bid to drown myself but Kurotimi wrestled me to the floor, in order to calm me down. He freed me after a while and I raced home like never before. The path home was silent as I couldn't hear anything on my way, with pace like that of a cheetah, I dashed the distance.

The moment I got home, everybody was crying. Seeing me, some people ran towards me to console me. Alas! I pushed them aside and ran straight inside the house to see the lifeless body of Chief Timipre Ngekpu Waibo, I lost consciousness.

The residence of Chief Ngekpu
Waibo.

I came around after a while and found
myself at a corner of our beautiful mud
house with palm fronds thatch,
surrounded by some youths of the
community led by Kurotimi. I broke free
from them and started searching for my
mother and younger brother,
Embelakpor. I found them behind the
compound in the company of some

5

women, I moved closer and wrapped them in my arms, consoling my mother.

[TWO MONTHS LATER, AFTER THE BURIAL OF MY FATHER]

Mama, **things go better, wo dau ogono emi owei, tari sai bo emi** [our father in heaven is bringing us blessings]. **Mopaa ine tubo, Ine koro bi di, kor kor, ari ine dau tubo eh** [Amen my son, look at your face, indeed you are the son of your father].
....

I continued farming in the land my father left behind as this was one thing I learnt from him. Farming became more interesting to me as it was a source of our livelihood; just that, this time, I was doing it without the presence and help of my father.

Seiyefa bagging his harvested cassava

God, make this year a better year, I know you will never forget me. Daddy, I will make sure your legacy remains and not go in vain.
I no sure say I go fit stop this cassava

business o, because my love for garri no get part two...

This is my business, garri plus soup equals balanced diet, garri plus beans equals balanced diet. **Who no work, no suppose chop o, if I no farm, I no suppose chop garri be that o...**

As I was thinking out loud, I burst into a tune,

My garri! My cassava! My garri! My cassava!
Oh groundnut! You go sweet for this my garri!
When I put River Niger water inside you,
Come add dicon salt, make I see if you no go rise,
And your current go flow inside my brain.

I remember whenever I sing this song, Embelakpor will burst into laughter, and then I will change the chorus,

My cassava, otaran [fufu],
My cassava, otaran[fufu],
If I knack am with better kirigina,
The cassava go know say na master handwork.

There are no dull moments whenever I am at the cassava farm.

Where those cassava groundnut when I pluck, make I use am soak my garri. E be like this my garri dey rise pass Ije own o? I said to myself.
The little cassava farm became so large. I harvested the cassava, peeled it, washed it and took it to the grinder for

9

grinding. After grinding, I mixed it with palm oil, since mama and papa love yellow garri so much. After mixing, I bagged it and left it with the grinder to dry it.

Pressing the cassava sack to drain the water in the garri.

I enjoyed frying garri so much. 'The internasunal [local accent] fryer [The international fryer]', my mother teased me like my father did. After frying, mama called me, and started praying for me. One thing I know my mother doesn't joke with is prayers, even though papa never believed in her prayers.

You no go lack anything for this life, I responded Amen
Your hard work go bring you plenty blessings anywhere you dey, I replied Amen.

After series of prayers, I took the garri to the market to sell, so we can have some money for the family upkeep and Embelakpor's school fees.

It was almost 4pm, that Monday evening at the market. I heard someone calling my name but it sounded different, it called out Saifar! Saifar! In my usual way, I didn't respond because of the fairy tale about spirits calling. Aside that, I said to myself, **my name no be Saifar, my name na Seiyefa, maybe na all this nonsense township people when don come market to buy our correct village product.**

Seiyefa selling at the market

As I was meditating, a customer came to me, requesting for two buckets of garri. The moment I was about putting the first bucket into the nylon for the customer, whom I had been admiring her daughter for years, someone held my hands, and in shock, the bucket of garri fell on the ground.

Bei ma titoru ese ama o? [What kind of trouble is this?]
I asked as I was raising my head to see who had held my hands and resulting in me pouring the garri on the floor...
Diimie!!! I shouted in excitement

Diimie replied, Saifar!
[The hailing continued in excitement]
Ari owei eh, Apo! kuro keme! bei ine koro Diimie?
[You are truly a man, strong man, is this you, Diimie?]

Diimie was just smiling at me as I was speaking our native dialect, I knew he must have forgotten how to speak but from his reactions, I sensed he could still understand. He was dumb to the language but not deaf.

Just then I heard a voice **Ari ma yerigha?** [Are you not selling anymore?], my crush's mother, Mrs Atangbala Korokumo, questioned.
Mummy, **pasise bolo kon kumo** [please don't be angry]
I apologized and sold the garri to her who still not aware of my crush on her daughter.

I used to wait for **Ebiere** (Good Girl), as I fondly teased her under that same mango tree, so I will tease her on her way to the river, whenever she went to

14

fetch water for her mother. Ebiere is so beautiful that one could lose concentration mere looking at her.

Mrs Atangbala handed me the money for the garri but I declined, saying, mummy, **bara siin** [mummy don't worry]. She thanked me and left.

At least, I had already sold about twenty bucket that day, which amounts to one hundred naira as each bucket cost five naira. It was from this money that Embelakpor's fees will be taken care of, and the family upkeep also.

I was still eager to catch up with my friend whom I haven't seen for more than fifteen years. We were only twelve years when Diimie left our community, **UBAKA** in **ODI KINGDOM.** We were like brothers, and my father was very fond of Diimie. Diimie usually spends majority of his time at our house after school, to the point that we were nicknamed **keni-mamu** [one and two]. During our secondary school, Diimie's father, Mr Wariebi Ebifegha, who was working at the post office won a US Lottery and took his family to the United States of America...

How's Dad? Diimie asked, looking into my eyes. I was silent for a moment, but before Diimie shouted Saifar, I broke in tears and summoned courage to tell him that papa is no more. Instantly, his countenance changed, I could see his eyes turning red, as if the oceans were about to overflow. This was one man Diimie loved and admired like his father. We held each other and consoled ourselves as we walked home.

We met mama in the kitchen, beside the beautiful mud house with palm fronds thatch. **zimie** [local accent for Diimie] as mama fondly called him due to our native tongue which was effective in my mother's speech. Mama was very excited, she held him to herself, and started talking **ine tubo, ine tubo, apo apo apo apo apo, abei, bei ine koro, ari duba sindo o, i dau a?**, [my child, is this your face, you are grown, how is your father?]. He replied mama saying they are fine and they sent their greetings, and some important messages. Mama smiled once more, as she said, '**make ona come inshide come sup the shweet kekefia and igina beni wey I make spesiallay.** [You guys should come and eat the delicious plantain porridge and pepper soup I prepared specially].

Diimie couldn't hold back his joy eating his favourite (local) delicacy, after so many years. You could see the excitement on his face as he rushed the food, so he could ask for more.

As we finished eating, Diimie asked after Embelakpor, my younger brother, but I cut him short before he could mistakenly ask after papa again, saying Embelakpor is in school. He then went to sit beside mama to console her, 'mama you are a strong woman, I heard what happened, mama, God will never forsake you because he will bless you more and more', Diimie went further to remind her that papa is with the Lord. Mama, I brought good news from my parents, Mama smiled, looking at Diimie... **gba ni dia ine tubo** [tell me, my child].

Diimie delivered the first envelope to Mama, bearing Papa's name – Mr Timipre Waibo, in as much as he is aware Mama could not read and write properly, but he did that as a sign of respect, and he presented another one bearing Mrs Imomotimi Waibo. He further presented the last envelope to me, bearing Embelakpor waibo. Papa's envelope contained ten thousand United States dollars, while mama's envelope contained eight thousand United States dollars and Embelakpor's was five thousand United States dollars.

Diimie said his dad holds dear the friendship between our both families, and it was a gift for a long time family that he hasn't forgotten and will never forget. His dad also promises to find time to visit soon. Mama opened the envelope and smiled, **which kind paper be this na my pikin?** Diimie and I burst into laughter, as we explained to Mama that it was the currency used in America.

Just then I looked at Diimie, he knew I wanted to ask for mine, but before I could say a word, he broke the news to us, Saifar! My father asked me to bring you along with me to Atlanta, so you won't be needing any dollars, as yours have been converted to further your education. For a minute I was no longer on planet earth, my eyes were bulging out as I heard Diimie say those words. I jumped up as if I was part of the team that represented Nigeria at the Olympics games in 1996 at Atlanta, Georgia, United States.

Mama started dancing and singing a song I haven't heard before [**bolo imbele imbele imbele, imbele lamo lamo, ingbai public holiday, public holiday** [great exceeding joy, today has been declared public holiday]. Indeed, great news is key to happiness. Joy filled our home.

After two months of preparation; traveling to Yenagoa to prepare International passport and also going to Lagos for my visa interview, it was time for Diimie and I to leave for Atlanta. Before we departed, Mama made starch and banga soup with lots of fresh fish and snail for myself and Diimie.

All vehicle arrangements were made at Kaiama, because we had to take a wooden boat to Kaiama. Mama, myself, Diimie and Embelakpor boarded the boat to Kaiama. On getting to Kaiama, Mama's tears were all over my shirt as she hugged me firmly. On the other end, Diimie was advising Embelakpor to be a good boy and to take care of Mama as he was now in charge of the cassava and garri family business. I promised Mama I was going to make her proud. Come here little boy, I spoke softly to my little brother, Embelakpor. I hugged him and told him to look after mama and never follow bad friends.

Mama, Seiyefa, Diimie and
Embel leaving for Kaiama

We bade ourselves farewell as Diimie
and I made our way to the vehicle
waiting to take us to Port-Harcourt
airport. We arrived Port-Harcourt
airport and quickly cleared our luggage
and all travel documents, and then we
proceeded to the Nigerian Airways
plane waiting for the passengers to
board.

23

'Diimie which kind thing be this na? see as e dey shake, my eyes dey turn me o', [what is happening, the plane is experiencing turbulence and its making me dizzy] I said as we were taking off. Diimie laughed and said to me, 'don't be afraid Saifar, it will take us safely to our destination. We got to Lagos after about 48 minutes. The landing was even scarier than the takeoff, I closed my eyes and prayed as the tyres hit the runway. We then waited for about an hour to get onboard our International flight.

Arriving at the J.F Kennedy international airport, Mr. and Mrs. Ebifegha were already waiting for us. Mrs. Ebifegha was so happy to see me as she held me tight speaking with an American accent, how are you doing Saifar, how is your mother, father and brother? As I was about answering, Diimie interrupted me and said they were fine, then Mr. Ebifegha grabbed me by my shoulder as we made our way to his vehicle.

After two months in the Atlanta, I finally got admitted into the prestigious George Washington University in DC to study Civil Engineering. It was difficult for me to cope as I couldn't understand the accent clearly but I tried my best to pay very detailed attention.

During the second year, I could understand the accent properly and my grades in school were very high. I told myself that I was going to make Mama and my late father proud by being outstanding. I studied daily, forgetting about parties and anything that will distract me from my academics.

Finally, I knew the hour had come as we began our final exams and writing my thesis wasn't easy, but determination and commitment kept me on track. After exams and defending my thesis, the results were out in less than a month, and to my greatest surprise, I was not only the best graduating student from my department, I was the second best graduating student from our set in the entire school.

After graduation, I was given a nice job, an apartment and a car by the American government to work at the White House. Mr. and Mrs. Ebifegha were proud of me, while I sent letters and money to Mama and Embelakpor, assuring them that I will be home soon. Sometimes Diimie will join me to work as it was an opportunity for him to enter the most revered 'white house.' My team was awarded contracts to carry out different projects severally.

Seiyefa's office at Washington DC.

After two years, I was able to set up my company in Washington DC, called SOB INNOVATIONS. A lot of people patronized me and gave me contracts like building hospital facilities and office space, which I carried out diligently with integrity and met all deadlines.

Finally, I knew it was time for me to visit Nigeria. I stopped by Mr. and Mrs. Ebifegha in company of their son Diimie, to inform them I was going to Nigeria to see my mother and Embelakpor and possibly bring them with me to Washington DC. Mr. and Mrs. Ebifegha prayed for me and wished me well. After which Diimie drove me to the airport.

News had already gotten to my mother that her son was coming home because I wrote them about my coming and made every arrangement for them to come to the airport.

...This is to announce the arrival of Nigerian Airways from the United States of America, according to Embelakpor, the voice over the PA system was sweet and lovely.

After twenty minutes of waiting, Embelakpor shouted, "Mama look at brother Seiyefa..." They made their way to the entrance of the arrival terminal and we hugged ourselves and walked towards the vehicle waiting to take us home. I had contacted a friend and colleague Tamara Adaka, whom I met at the university to build for me a modern smart house. I knew him to be a truthful person all through our stay at the university, and he was from our neighboring community, Kaiama. On our way home, Mama was asking a lot of questions that I couldn't answer because before I could finish answering one, Mama will throw another out of excitement.

Getting to the duplex, mama asked again, **bei tubaki wari o?** [whose house is this?], Seiyefa, I replied, mama **inei** [mama, it is mine] Mama knew I was doing well, because the Nigerian government had spoken so well about me, that a Nigerian called Seiyefa Waibo is making them proud in the White House, Washington and Magazines and other media had published reports about me.

During my stay in Nigeria, I was making arrangements for my mother and Embelakpor to join me on my way back, while I tried setting up SOB INNOVATONS in Port-Harcourt with the help of Tamara Adaka.

Finally, we were able to set the plan for the company and conducted recruitments. Tamara assured me that he will do everything to make SOB INNOVATIONS a household name in Nigeria.

It was time to leave for United State of America, as my vacation was over. Tamara drove us to the airport, I could see the smile on Embelakpor's face, because he has heard a lot about America. Mama was smiling too as we were boarding the airline.

Mama, Seiyefa and
Embelakpor leaving for
United States of America

...Fasten your seat belts, said the pilot, just as I was assisting Mama and Embelakpor with their belts, Mama looked at me and said, **I dey proud for you, shun**. [I am proud of you, my son]. You could hear the sound of the engine as the plane sped on the runway, Embelakpor whispered to me with a smile on his face, 'America here I come', I laughed and said to myself, 'Indeed, **God can bless anybody, just always believe in God and keep doing your best, he will give you your heart desires**.